STICKS
and
STONES

(Reflection Journal)

Tee Soulful

Page intentionally left blank

Copyrights

Dedication

Dedicated to my son Zion who is the drive behind me writing this book. You can do anything no matter what.

Acknowledgement

To be provided by the client.

About the Author

Born and raised in Toronto, in one of the city's tougher neighborhoods, Tricia learned early what resilience truly means. Refusing to let circumstances define the limits of possibility, she turned challenges into motivation, proving wrong those who doubted her potential including teachers who once told her otherwise.

Driven by curiosity and a love for language, Tricia aka Tee Soulful traveled the world, teaching English both online and in classrooms across diverse cultures. Each destination added a new perspective, shaping a deeper understanding of people, perseverance, and purpose.

Through every setback and success, one constant remained my son, whose belief and encouragement became the ultimate inspiration to keep "beating this game called life."

Table of Contents

CHAPTER 1 Zayla's Monday Mood 1

CHAPTER 2 The Friendship Test 3

CHAPTER 3 The Rumor Rumble 6

CHAPTER 4 The Stand-up Surprise 8

CHAPTER 5 The Friendship Test 11

CHAPTER 6 The Bounce-Back Plan 14

CHAPTER 7 Rumor Shield Activated 17

CHAPTER 8 The Power of "No Thanks" 20

CHAPTER 9 The Kindness Ripple 23

CHAPTER 10 When Whispers Get Loud 26

CHAPTER 11 The Power of One 29

CHAPTER 12 The Mirror Test................................32

CHAPTER 13 Operation Speak-Up...................35

CHAPTER 14 The Compliment Chain..........................39

CHAPTER 15 The Great Misunderstanding................43

CHAPTER 16 The Secret Handshake...........................48

CHAPTER 17 The Big Switch....................................52

CHAPTER 18 The Lost Lunch.................................59

CHAPTER 19 The Unexpected Apology.....................64

CHAPTER 20 The Strength to Walk Away................69

CHAPTER 21 Rumors are like Tornadoes...................75

CHAPTER 22 Kindness: Real Superpower.................83

CHAPTER 23 When They Go Low You Go High.......87

CHAPTER 24 You're Not Alone..................................92

CHAPTER 25 Stronger Than You Think......................97

CHAPTER 26 Lifting Others................................ 101

CHAPTER 27 The Pause of Pause 105

CHAPTER 28 One Compliment Can Change Everything.. 109

CHAPTER 29 The Day Zayla Messed Up 112

CHAPTER 30 The Big Test................................... 115

CHAPTER 31 Not for Sale.................................. 119

CHAPTER 32 The Ripple Effect 123

CHAPTER 33 Locker Notes and Lemonade 126

CHAPTER 34 The Apology Circle......................... 130

CHAPTER 35 Change Starts Quietly 134

CHAPTER 36 The New Kid Rule 138

CHAPTER 37 Even Heroes Need Help 143

CHAPTER 38 Different, Not Less 148

CHAPTER 39 The Apology Circle 153

CHAPTER 40 This Is Just the Beginning 158

CHAPTER 1

Zayla's Monday Mood

Zayla didn't want to get out of bed. Not because she was tired. But because middle school drama was real... and sticky... like gum in your hair.

She pulled the blanket over her head and whispered, "If I can't see them, they can't see me."

Unfortunately, that spell never worked.

Her mom shouted from downstairs, "Zayla! If you miss that bus again, you're going to be walking to school with the raccoons!"

Zayla sighed. The raccoons were probably more chill than some of the girls in her homeroom.

She slid out of bed, hoodie first, hair doing its own thing, and grabbed her backpack. Inside: one broken pencil, a crushed snack bar, and exactly zero energy for gossip.

CHAPTER 2

The Friendship Test

Zayla thought today might actually be normal. She had new shoes (finally), a backpack that wasn't ripped (yet), and a solid plan not to trip going up the stairs.

Things were looking up... until she met Maya.

Maya was one of those kids who seemed cool without even trying. She had sparkly nails, a high ponytail, and an entire posse that laughed at everything she said, even when it wasn't funny.

At lunch, Maya waved Zayla over. "Hey, want to sit with us?" she said, smiling like she meant it. Zayla's heart did a backflip. Finally! A real friend!

She squeezed into the seat next to Maya, clutching her sad little sandwich like a life raft. That's when Maya leaned in and whispered, "If you want to be part of the group, you have to pass the Friendship Test."

Zayla blinked. "The what-now?" Maya grinned. "Simple. You have to balance a banana on your head and walk across the cafeteria." Zayla looked down. No banana. No instructions. No emergency exit.

Her brain scrambled: Maybe it's just a joke? Maybe it's a secret test to see if I'm brave? Maybe this is how friendships work? But deep down, Zayla knew: Real friends don't make you feel small. Real friends don't make you earn a seat at the table.

She smiled a real one this time and shook her head. "I'm good. I already passed my real test today... getting out of bed." She picked up her tray and moved to a different table, a wobbly one, next to a kid drawing cartoons on a napkin.

It wasn't perfect. But it was real. And sometimes real is even better than cool. Your Turn: The Friendship Test. Think about it: Have you ever felt like you had to prove yourself just to fit in? Maybe someone dared you to do something silly... or made you feel like you weren't good enough?

Write about it below!

- What happened?
- How did it make you feel?
- What would you tell someone else going through the same thing?

CHAPTER 3

The Rumor Rumble

It started with a whisper... and somehow ended with Zayla "supposedly" owning a pet snake that ate homework. Which she absolutely did not, although it would've been cool.

By lunchtime, half the school was whispering. Some kids pointed. Some giggled. A few even backed away slowly, like Zayla was carrying a monster in her backpack.

At first, she tried laughing it off, but by 2:00 p.m., it wasn't funny anymore. It felt like no matter where she went, boom, someone was talking about her. Like she had suddenly become a walking headline in a newspaper nobody asked for. That's the thing about rumors: They don't need to be true. They just need one person brave enough to say, "Hey, that's not cool."

Unfortunately... nobody did. Not yet, anyway.

CHAPTER 4

The Stand-up Surprise

Zayla was minding her own business when it happened. She was reaching into her locker, humming a random tune, when she heard it.

"Hey, Snake Girl!" someone snickered down the hall. Pause. Deep breath. Stay cool.

Zayla knew she had two choices:

Pretend she didn't hear it and shrink into her hoodie like a turtle, turn around, and launch a glitter cannon of comebacks.

She was leaning toward Option #2 when something shocking happened... Somebody else spoke up first. "Dude, that's not funny. Leave her alone," said a voice from across the hallway. It was Jonas, a kid who usually kept to himself, more into drawing superheroes than being one.

Everyone froze like someone had hit a giant PAUSE button on the whole school. Even the kid who said it looked stunned, like he didn't expect anyone to care.

Zayla blinked. Was she dreaming? Nope. Jonas just shrugged, popped his earbuds back in, and walked away like it was no big deal. But it was a big deal.

Maybe standing up didn't always mean making a huge speech. Maybe sometimes it just meant saying what's right... and moving on.

Reflection Time:

- Have you ever seen someone stand up for another person?
- How did it change the situation?
- What's one small thing you could do if you see someone being picked on?

Draw a "hero badge" for someone who stands up for others!

CHAPTER 5

The Friendship Test

After the whole Snake Girl thing, Zayla started paying more attention, not to the bullies, but to her friends.

Turns out, a real friend doesn't disappear when rumors fly. A real friend doesn't suddenly act like they don't know you just because some bored kids need a new hobby.

At lunch, Zayla sat down at her usual table. Maya smiled and scooted over. "Saved you a seat," she said like nothing weird had happened all day.

Meanwhile, Jade, who had been Zayla's partner-in-laughs since forever, just... stared at her tray. Picked at her food. Whispered with other girls and didn't even look up.

Ouch.

It wasn't like a punch in the face. It was more like a slow leak, a friendship balloon quietly losing air, and you know what? Sometimes that's how you find out who's really riding with you… And who's just along for the snacks. Zayla took a deep breath, smiled at Maya, and decided: Quality over quantity. Always.

Reflection Time:

- How do you know when someone is a real friend?
- Have you ever had a friendship "pop" when you didn't expect it?
- What's one thing you can do to be a strong friend for somebody else?

Draw two friends riding skateboards together. One falls, the other helps them up!

CHAPTER 6

The Bounce-Back Plan

Zayla could've stayed stuck. She could've stayed mad, stayed quiet, stayed small.

But guess what? That's not how bounce-backs work.

Bounce-backs are messy. Bounce-backs are loud. Bounce-backs sometimes start with crying into your pillow... and end with you building a life ten times cooler than before.

So, Zayla made a plan.

Step 1: Find her people. Not the fake smilers. Not the "I 'll-text-you-later" ghosts. Her real people. The ones who laughed with her, not at her.

Step 2: Do her thing. She loved art. She loved music. She loved inventing weird milkshake flavors (pickle-banana, anyone?). She wasn't going to quit being awesome just because someone else couldn't see it.

Step 3: Walk like she owned the hallway. Even if her backpack was sliding off one shoulder. Even if her shoelace was untied. Even if she secretly wanted to run home and hide under the covers.

Stick and Stones

Confidence isn't about feeling brave all the time. It's about walking through the hallway anyway.

Reflection Time:

- When was a time you felt knocked down but got back up?
- Who are your "real people," the ones who cheer for you even on your worst days?
- What's your favorite "bounce-back" song that makes you feel invincible?

On a separate piece of paper, draw yourself wearing an invisible superhero cape. What does it look like?

CHAPTER 7

Rumor Shield Activated

You know what's faster than a cheetah? Faster than Wi-Fi? A good, juicy rumor.

By the time Zayla got to the third period, there were already whispers. By lunch? Full-blown soap opera.

According to the hallways, Zayla had:

- Stole someone's hamster.
- Been suspended for throwing spaghetti in the cafeteria.
- Joined a secret dance crew (okay, that one sounded kind of cool).

At first, her stomach twisted up like a pretzel. How do you fight a million rumors at once?

Answer: You don't. You shield up.

Zayla pretended every mean whisper was a dodgeball, and every time one flew at her, she dodged it, swatted it, shrugged it off.

Because the truth was her shield. And the people who mattered? They knew who she really was.

Rumors were just noise. And Zayla decided she had better things to do than dance with noise. Like her story. Not someone else's version of it.

Reflection Time:

- Have you ever had a rumor spread about you or someone you know?
- What helped you handle it, or what would help next time?
- Why is it important to stay true to yourself when others are talking?

Stick and Stones

On a separate piece of paper, draw yourself holding a giant shield with your favorite powerful word written across it (like "BRAVE" or "STRONG").

CHAPTER 8

The Power of "No Thanks"

Zayla used to think she had to say yes to everything. Yes, to friends who made her feel small. Yes to jokes that weren't funny. Yes to plans she didn't even like.

Because if she said no... would they still like her?

Spoiler alert: Real friends don't vanish when you say "no thanks."

One Friday afternoon, the so-called "cool crew" invited her to a group chat full of jokes about other kids. Laughing at clothes. Laughing at hair. Laughing at dreams.

It was the kind of invitation Zayla would've jumped at last year.

But not today. Today, she pictured her invisible superhero cape. She pictured her shield.

And she typed two words, "No thanks."

Simple. Strong. Done.

Did it feel scary? A little. Did it feel powerful? A LOT.

That tiny "no thanks" wasn't tiny at all. It was a huge YES to herself.

Reflection Time:

- Have you ever said "no thanks" to something that didn't feel right?
- How did it feel afterward?
- Why is it important to choose friends who lift you up, not tear others down?

Draw a superhero badge with the word "NO" in the center like a powerful emblem.

CHAPTER 9

The Kindness Ripple

Zayla had figured out something big. You know those moments when you do something nice and it feels... amazing? Like, you give someone a compliment and watch their face light up.

What if that feeling could spread? What if you could create a ripple of kindness, like tossing a pebble into a calm lake, and it just keeps spreading outward?

Zayla decided to test it.

Instead of joining the gossip circle at lunch, she smiled at the kid sitting alone in the corner. "Hey, I like your hoodie. It's got cool colors," she said.

The kid smiled back, a little confused but happy. Zayla didn't need to start a full-on friendship, just a small, simple act of kindness.

Then, later, she saw Maya help someone with their homework. And the kid who smiled at Zayla helped pick up a pencil for someone who'd dropped it.

It wasn't huge. But the ripple was growing.

Zayla realized that kindness wasn't about grand gestures. It was about creating little waves that added up to something powerful.

Reflection Time:

- What's the last kind thing someone did for you?
- How did it make you feel?
- What's one small act of kindness you could do tomorrow?

Draw a ripple effect starting with a kind word you said, and how it spreads out!

CHAPTER 10

When Whispers Get Loud

At first, it was just whispers. Tiny, slithery sounds behind Zayla's back.

"She thinks she's better than us." "She's too good." "She's fake nice."

Zayla heard them, not with her ears but with her heart.

The old Zayla would have cried in the bathroom stall. The new Zayla? She was hurt... but stronger. Because now she knew: When people whispered about you, it said more about them than it ever said about you.

Whispers are weak. Kindness is loud.

Instead of shrinking, Zayla did the unthinkable: She stood even taller.

She helped even more. She laughed even louder. She stayed exactly who she was.

By the end of the week, the whispers started shrinking. People saw that being real was way cooler than being cruel.

Zayla didn't need to fight whispers with whispers. She fought them by living loud.

Reflection Time:

- Has someone ever whispered about you or someone else behind their back?
- What's one positive thing you can say out loud instead?
- Why is it stronger to be kind than to be mean?

Draw a cartoon of yourself with a giant microphone that says "Kindness" on it, blasting over tiny whispers!

CHAPTER 11

The Power of One

Sometimes it felt like the whole school was on one team... and Zayla was on the other. One girl against a sea of rumors, jokes, and eye-rolls.

But then she remembered something her grandma once said: "It only takes one candle to light up a whole room."

One voice to speak up. One smile to change a day. One act of kindness to flip the whole story.

Zayla decided she would be that one.

At lunch, she invited someone new to sit with her, even when her hands were shaking. In gym class, she cheered for the quiet kid who always got picked last. In the hallway, she smiled at the girl who wore the same hoodie every day.

None of it made her famous. None of it made her "cool." It made her brave, and little by little, other candles lit up too. Small sparks, big difference.

Zayla learned you don't need a whole crowd to change things. You just need one brave heart to start.

Reflection Time:

- Have you ever been the "only one" who did the right thing? How did it feel?
- What's one brave thing you could do this week to stand up for kindness?

Draw yourself holding a candle that lights up a dark room, and then show others joining with their own candles!

CHAPTER 12

The Mirror Test

Zayla used to stare into the mirror and ask the wrong questions: "Why me?" "Why can't I just fit in?" "What's wrong with me?"

But after everything she had been through, the whispers, the looks, the tests of her kindness, Zayla learned to ask a better question:

"What's right with me?"

Every morning, she looked into the mirror and named one thing: "I'm kind." "I'm strong." "I'm a good friend." "I'm brave, even when it's hard."

The mirror didn't change. Zayla did.

She realized that sometimes people threw stones because they didn't like their own reflections. Their words weren't about her. They were about them. And Zayla? She wasn't going to let anyone else's broken mirror break her spirit.

From that day on, the most important opinion about Zayla... Was Zayla's.

Reflection Time:

- What is one GOOD thing you can say about yourself today?
- Why is it important to believe in yourself even when others don't?

Draw a mirror and inside it, write words that describe your BEST qualities!

CHAPTER 13

Operation Speak-Up

Zayla never liked raising her hand in class. Her voice always felt too small, like a whisper lost in a thunderstorm. What if she said the wrong answer? What if they laughed?

One day, Mrs. Simmons, Zayla's teacher, wrote two words on the board:

"BRAVE MOMENTS."

She told the class, "Being brave isn't about being loud. It's about showing up anyway."

Mrs. Simmons gave everyone a secret mission: Each student had to complete one brave moment before the end of the week.

Some kids planned to give a speech. Some were going to sing. Some even thought about telling a joke during lunch.

Zayla thought long and hard. Maybe... Maybe her brave moment could be something small like raising her hand.

The next morning, Zayla sat with her heart thumping like a bass drum. Her palms were sweaty. But when Mrs. Simmons asked, "Who wants to share?"...

Zayla's hand shot up even before her brain had time to argue.

Mrs. Simmons smiled. The class leaned in.

Zayla's voice wobbled a little, but it came out clear: "I think... It's okay to be different. It makes us interesting."

There was a pause. Then claps. Big ones.

Zayla didn't need to be the loudest. She just needed to believe in her voice.

And in that moment... she did. Mission complete.

Reflection Time:

- What would YOUR brave moment be?
- Can you think of a time you spoke up, even when you were scared?

Draw a comic strip showing yourself completing a Brave Moment!

CHAPTER 14

The Compliment Chain

After her "brave moment," Zayla felt like a new person. Not louder. Not bolder. Just... more herself.

At lunch the next day, her friend Mia said, "You know, you have the best laugh. It makes people feel happy."

Zayla blinked. No one had ever said that to her before. It felt nice. Warm, like a cozy sweater.

So, Zayla passed it on. She turned to the boy sitting across from her, Liam, and said, "You're really good at building stuff in art class. Your cardboard castle was epic."

Liam turned red and beamed.

Then he passed it on. And so did the next person. And the next.

By the end of lunch, it was like compliments were flying across the room like snowballs, but the good kind that melted right into your heart.

Someone even said the meanest girl in school had cool shoes. And you know what? They were pretty cool.

Zayla learned something big that day: Kindness is contagious. One small spark could start a wildfire, a GOOD one.

Stick and Stones

Reflection Time:

- Have you ever given someone a compliment and seen their whole face light up?
- What's a compliment someone gave you that you'll never forget?

Design a "Kindness Badge" that you would give to someone today!

CHAPTER 15

The Great Misunderstanding

It started with a whisper.

Zayla had barely walked through the school doors when she heard her name float through the hallway like smoke.

"Zayla did what?" "No way. I heard it too!"

Her steps slowed. Her stomach twisted. She felt everyone's eyes on her, or maybe she just imagined it. Either way, it was that awful feeling… like something was wrong, but no one would say it out loud.

Her first thought was to hide. Her second thought was to shout, "It's not true!"

But instead, she paused and took a deep breath. She remembered something her teacher once said: **"Don't add fuel to the fire. Bring water instead."**

So, Zayla didn't run. She didn't cry. She found out who had started the story, a girl named Lani, who was leaning against her locker, texting with one hand and whispering to a friend with the other.

Zayla walked right up to her and smiled calmly.

"Hey," she said. "I've been hearing some pretty wild things about me this morning. Mind if we talk?"

Lani froze. Her thumb hovered over her phone screen. She glanced up, surprised.

"I—uh—what?" Lani said, suddenly unsure of herself.

Zayla didn't accuse. She didn't raise her voice. She just stood there, calm but strong.

"I just figured we could clear it up," Zayla said. "Because the stuff going around... It's not true. And I know how things can get twisted fast."

Lani hesitated… and then shrugged. "Honestly? I didn't mean for it to spread. Someone told me you said something about skipping class, and then I told Maya, and then… I guess it got big."

"Like a game of Telephone," Zayla said with a small smile.

Lani laughed a little nervously. "Yeah. Kind of blew up, huh?"

They ended up walking to class together, both a little surprised at how easy it had been to talk it out.

By the time the final bell rang that day, the rumor had already lost its power.

No drama. No yelling. Just the truth calmly spoken.

Zayla learned something important that day:

You don't always have to fight fire with fire. Sometimes, the strongest move is to face the storm with calm confidence… and clear the air, one real conversation at a time.

Reflection

1. What happened to Zayla at the beginning of the chapter?

2. How did Zayla choose to respond to the rumor?

3. What did Zayla learn after talking to the girl?

4. What was the result of Zayla's calm approach?

5. What is the main lesson from this chapter

CHAPTER 16

The Secret Handshake

After everything that had happened, Zayla and her friends realized something important: they wanted a way to show they always had each other's backs, not just with words, but with something fun, creative, and just for them.

So, one afternoon during lunch, they sat in a circle and came up with an idea: The Ultimate Friendship Handshake.

It wasn't just any handshake. It had three high-fives (to celebrate each other), a cool spin move (to show their energy and uniqueness), and a pretend crown placed on each other's heads at the end (to remind each other of their worth like royalty).

They practiced it over and over, laughing every time someone messed up the spin or forgot the crown. But soon, they had it down perfectly.

That handshake became more than just a game; it became a symbol.

Anyone who learned it became part of their group, which they proudly called the "No Bully Zone Club." It wasn't about excluding others. In fact, it was the opposite. It was about making sure everyone felt included, safe, and supported.

Whenever someone had a rough day, felt left out, or just needed a boost, one of the friends would walk up and say nothing, just hold out a hand. Then came the handshake. And just like that: BAM instant smile. No explanations. No long talks. Just the unspoken message: "You're not alone."

It was their secret code. Their badge of friendship. And a reminder that sometimes, a single gesture can say more than a hundred words.

Reflection

1. Why did Zayla and her friends decide to create a secret handshake?

2. What were the parts of the "Ultimate Friendship Handshake"? List them.

3. What did the "No Bully Zone Club" stand for?

4. How did the handshake help someone who was feeling down?

5. What is the main lesson from this chapter?

6. Think and Respond: What's something small you could create or do with your friends to show support, like Zayla's handshake?

CHAPTER 17

The Big Switch

It started like any other Tuesday: gray skies, lukewarm oatmeal in the cafeteria, and the usual chatter as students filed into Room 204. But then Mrs. Simmons clapped her hands and grinned.

"I have a surprise," she said.

The room fell silent. Mrs. Simmons' surprises could go either way: last month, it was a pop quiz; the month before, a pajama day.

"Today, we're switching seats!"

Cue the groans, moans, and a synchronized wave of eye-rolls.

Zayla slumped in her chair. She liked her desk. It was perfectly positioned next to the window and just far enough from the board that she didn't have to worry about Mrs.

Simmons seeing her doodles. Most importantly, she sat next to Maya, her best friend forever.

Now, everything was being rearranged.

By the time the dust settled and the last backpack was scooted under a new desk, Zayla found herself seated next to Ben.

Ben, who never raised his hand. Ben, who always looked like he'd rather be anywhere else. Ben, who once growled when someone borrowed his ruler.

Zayla sighed. This was going to be the worst week ever.

At first, they barely spoke. She worked on her spelling, and he scribbled in a worn black notebook filled with tiny sketches and strange notes.

On Wednesday, during science class, they were paired up for the "Volcanic Eruption" project. Zayla tried to offer ideas, but Ben only nodded or shrugged.

But then something changed.

Thursday afternoon, Zayla noticed Ben carefully mixing vinegar and baking soda with exact measurements. He muttered something about "pressure release ratios." Intrigued, she leaned in.

"Wait... you built that model yourself?" she asked.

Ben blinked. "Yeah," he said. "Want to help me make it erupt?"

They spent the rest of the afternoon laughing over eruptions gone wrong once, their papier-mâché volcano leaked out the side and fizzed all over Ben's math homework.

Finally, Friday arrived. The big presentation day.

Zayla and Ben stood in front of the class as Mrs. Simmons counted down. "Three... two... one..."

BOOM! The volcano erupted in a glorious, foamy burst of lava-colored fizz that shot three feet in the air.

The class gasped. Some cheered. Mrs. Simmons clapped.

Zayla grinned at Ben. "That was awesome!"

Ben smiled, really smiled for the first time all week. "Yeah," he said. "Thanks for helping."

By the end of the day, they were swapping favorite science facts and planning what to build next. Zayla realized something surprising:

Ben wasn't grumpy. He was just shy... and really, really smart.

Sometimes, all it takes is one small switch to spark a big friendship.

- Draw a picture of Zayla and Ben's erupting volcano!
- Write a letter to Zayla giving her advice about her new friendship with Ben.
- Finish this sentence: "Sometimes, when you take a chance and try something new…"

Reflection Page

Think about it…

1. **First Impressions:**

At the beginning of the chapter, Zayla had a strong opinion about Ben.

➤ Why do you think she felt that way?

➤ Have you ever made a quick judgment about someone that turned out to be wrong?

2. **Change and Surprise:**

Mrs. Simmons made the class switch seats, and that led to a big change for Zayla.

➤ Why do you think it's hard for people to try something new, like changing seats or working with someone different?

➤ What surprised Zayla the most about Ben?

3. Teamwork and Discovery:

Zayla and Ben built something great together.

➤ What did they learn about each other during the science project?

➤ How did working together help them both grow?

4. Friendship in Unexpected Places:

➤ What does this chapter teach us about friendship?

➤ Can you think of someone you didn't know very well at first, but who later became a friend

C

CHAPTER 18

The Lost Lunch

It was just a regular recess, sunny sky, jump ropes slapping pavement, the smell of peanut butter and jelly drifting from lunchboxes.

Zayla was halfway through her sandwich, chatting with a group of classmates, when she noticed someone sitting alone under the big oak tree near the edge of the playground.

It was Jayden, a quiet kid who had joined their class a few weeks ago but barely spoke to anyone. He sat cross-legged, holding an old brown paper bag. As he opened it, Zayla saw him pull out… a single, bruised apple. No sandwich. No snacks. Not even a drink.

Jayden poked at the apple with his finger. He didn't look sad, exactly, just used to it, like this was normal.

Zayla didn't think. She just acted.

She tore her sandwich in half, wrapped one piece in a napkin from her lunchbox, and walked over. "Hey," she said softly, holding it out. "You want some?"

Jayden blinked. For a second, he didn't move. Then he took the sandwich, nodded, and gave a tiny smile that barely reached the corners of his mouth.

He didn't say anything.

But the next day at lunch, Jayden slid his tray onto the bench beside Zayla. This time, it was a full sandwich, chips, juice, and… two cookies.

He handed one to Zayla without a word.

They didn't talk much. They didn't have to.

Some friendships begin not with big conversations, but with small kindnesses, the kind that ripple, echoing further than you ever expect.

Reflection Page

1. What does Zayla's action tell us about her character? Think about how she responded to seeing Jayden alone with very little to eat.

➤ Was she trying to be a hero, or just being kind?

➤ Have you ever helped someone in a quiet way like this?

2. Why do you think Jayden didn't say much?

➤ How can people show appreciation even if they don't use words?

➤ What does his cookie-sharing the next day say about how he felt?

3. What do you think the line "Small kindnesses echo louder than you think" means?

➤ Can one small act really make a big difference in someone's day… or even their life?

➤ Why are quiet moments of kindness sometimes the most powerful?

CHAPTER 19

The Unexpected Apology

Sometimes, people surprise you in the most unexpected ways, on the most ordinary days.

It was a Thursday afternoon, just after art class. The bell had rung, backpacks were being zipped, and the halls buzzed with chatter as students poured out of Room 204.

Zayla was grabbing her sketchbook from her cubby when she heard a voice behind her.

"Hey… Zayla?"

She turned and blinked. It was Sasha, the girl who, just a few months ago, had called her "Try-Hard Zayla" in front of everyone during gym. The same Sasha who rolled her eyes when Zayla answered questions in class, who once made fun of her shoes, who always seemed to have something mean to say.

Zayla braced herself.

But Sasha didn't look smug or mean today. In fact, she looked… nervous.

She shuffled her feet and stared at the floor. "I… I just wanted to say I'm sorry," Sasha mumbled.

Zayla blinked. "For what?"

Sasha shrugged, her voice quiet. "For how I treated you before. I didn't mean to be so mean. I guess… I guess I was just kind of jealous."

There it was. The truth. No excuses, no drama, just honesty.

Zayla stood there, unsure what to say. Part of her still remembered the sting of Sasha's words, the heat of embarrassment, the way she avoided Sasha in the hallways.

But another part of her, a quieter part, understood.

People make mistakes. Sometimes big ones.

So, she just nodded.

"Okay," Zayla said softly. "Thanks for saying that."

Sasha gave a half-smile, then walked away. They didn't suddenly become friends. They didn't sit together at lunch or pass notes during math.

But something did change.

After that day, Sasha stopped being cruel. She wasn't overly friendly, but she was polite. Respectful. And sometimes, that's enough.

Zayla realized that forgiving someone didn't mean pretending it never happened. It didn't erase the hurt or make them best friends.

But it did mean she didn't have to carry the weight of someone else's anger anymore.

Forgiveness wasn't for Sasha. It was for herself a way to let go, breathe easier, and walk forward without looking back.

Reflection Page

1. What do you think made Sasha decide to apologize?

➤ Do you think it was easy or hard for her to say "I'm sorry"? Why?

➤ Have you ever had to apologize for something that took a lot of courage?

2. How did Zayla respond to Sasha's apology, and what does that say about her?

➤ Why didn't she get angry or bring up the past?

➤ What does it mean to forgive someone without becoming close friends afterward?

3. "Forgiveness didn't mean forgetting — it just meant Zayla could move forward without carrying someone else's anger on her back."

➤ What do you think this sentence means?

➤ Have you ever felt better after forgiving someone — even if they never said sorry?

Write about a time when someone surprised you with kindness or honesty.

Imagine you're Sasha. Write a short journal entry about why you decided to say sorry to Zayla.

Finish this sentence: "Forgiving someone doesn't change the past, but it helps me…"

CHAPTER 20

The Strength to Walk Away

Sometimes, the bravest thing you can do isn't shouting.

It isn't standing tall with your fists clenched or proving someone wrong.

Sometimes, real strength… is walking away.

Zayla learned that one warm afternoon during lunch break.

She was on her way to the swings when she heard voices behind the gym, loud, teasing ones. She peeked around the corner and saw a group of kids pointing and laughing at another student, Riley. Riley had on mismatched socks, a wrinkled shirt, and shoes that were clearly too small.

The kids were snickering.

"Nice outfit," one of them said with a fake smile.

"Where'd you get those shoes? A time machine from the '90s?" another added.

Zayla felt her fists tighten. Her heart beat faster. She hated bullying. She wanted to yell, to jump in, to tell them all to stop.

But then… she paused.

She remembered something important. She had learned it from her mom, from books, from her own growing-up:

Not every fight is worth your energy.

Instead of getting loud or angry, Zayla took a deep breath. She walked straight up to Riley, ignoring the group completely.

She gently took Riley's hand and said, "Come on. Let's go."

Riley looked surprised, then grateful. The two of them turned and walked away. No yelling. No tears. No drama.

Just… quiet power.

Behind them, the bullies were left standing awkwardly, their jokes falling flat. Without an audience, they looked less cool and more like kids trying too hard to be mean.

As they reached the playground, Riley whispered, "Thanks."

Zayla smiled. "You don't have to stay where people don't treat you right."

That day, Zayla learned something big:

Sometimes, you don't win by shouting.

Sometimes, you win by choosing peace.

You win by walking away… and by showing someone else how to walk with you.

Reflection Page

1. Why do you think Zayla chose not to yell at the bullies?

➤ What might have happened if she had?

➤ What does her choice say about her strength and maturity?

2. What impact did Zayla's quiet action have on Riley and the bullies?

➤ Why was simply walking away so powerful in that moment?

➤ Have you ever seen someone help in a calm, quiet way? What did it look like?

3.   "Sometimes you win by not playing their game."

➤What do you think this means?

➤ Can you think of a time when walking away or staying calm helped you avoid making a situation worse?

CHAPTER 21

Rumors are like Tornadoes

Rumors are sneaky.

They don't stomp in loudly or wave their arms to get your attention.

They start small, like a soft breeze whispering in the hallways.

But if people repeat them, even just once...

If they pass them along without thinking...

That breeze turns into wind.

And that wind turns into a storm.

And before long, it's spinning so fast, no one knows what's true anymore.

It becomes a tornado, loud, messy, and full of hurt.

Tee Soulful

One Thursday morning, Zayla walked into class and felt something strange in the air. People were whispering. Heads were turning. Some kids were snickering behind their hands.

"Did you hear what Leo did?" someone whispered near her desk.

Zayla froze.

Leo was her friend. They built LEGO cities together during free time and shared popcorn on movie days. Zayla knew him well — and she knew the story floating around didn't sound like him at all.

She listened for a moment. The rumor was wild — too wild to be true. And even worse, people were repeating it without checking the facts.

Zayla felt her stomach twist.

She didn't like drama. But she liked lies even less.

Stick and Stones

So, she stood up, calmly and clearly, and said:

"Unless you heard it from Leo, I don't want to hear it at all."

The group around her fell silent.

One kid blinked. Another fidgeted. No one expected Zayla — quiet, creative, always-drawing-Zayla — to speak up like that.

But she did.

And in that moment, it felt like the storm stopped spinning.

The tornado started to fade.

By lunchtime, no one was whispering about Leo anymore.

The rumor fizzled out before it could grow bigger, before it could hurt him.

Later that day, Leo thanked her.

"I don't even know what they were saying," he said. "But I'm glad you had my back."

Zayla smiled. "That's what friends do."

She walked home that day feeling tall. Not because she yelled or fought — but because she stood for something.

Stopping a rumor doesn't take superpowers.

Just courage, kindness, and a voice strong enough to say:

"That's not okay."

 Reflection Page

Theme: Truth, Courage, and the Power of One Voice

💬 Think About It

1. Why do rumors spread so easily — even when they're not true?

➤ What makes people want to repeat something juicy or dramatic?

➤ How can even small rumors grow into something much more hurtful?

Sentence Starter: Rumors grow when people…

2. How did Zayla stop the rumor without being mean or dramatic?

➤ What did she say, and why was it effective?

➤ What message did she send to her classmates by speaking up?

Sentence Starter: Zayla stopped the rumor by…

3. What can you do if you hear a rumor about someone you care about (or even someone you don't know well)?

➤ What's the kindest and bravest thing you could do in that moment?

➤ How might your words or silence affect the person being talked about?

Sentence Starter: Next time I hear a rumor, I will…

Journal Prompt #1: Write about a time you heard something that might not have been true.

- What did you do?
- How did it make you feel?
- Would you do anything differently now?

Journal Prompt #2: Pretend you're Leo. Write a journal entry about how it felt to know a rumor was spreading — and how it felt when Zayla stood up for you.

Journal Prompt #3: Make a list of rumor-stopping superpowers — things anyone can do to calm a situation instead of making it worse. For example:

- Ask, "Is that true?"
- Say, "That's not kind."
- Walk away.
- Tell a teacher or adult.

🎨 Creative Corner

- Draw a tornado on one side of a page. On the other hand, draw Zayla standing strong like a superhero, using her words to calm the wind.

- Create a mini poster that says: **"Unless you heard it from them, don't pass it on."** Decorate it with symbols of truth, peace, or bravery.

CHAPTER 22

Kindness: Real Superpower

Some people think you need a cape to be a hero.

Or muscles. Or magic. Or a giant roar that makes people listen.

But Zayla learned something different.

Something better.

Kindness, quiet, real kindness, is the strongest superpower of all.

It was a chilly Monday when Ava arrived at school.

She was new. She was quiet. She wore scuffed-up sneakers and carried a backpack that looked like it had been through one too many rainy days.

By lunchtime, the whispers had started.

"Did you see her shoes?"

"That backpack is falling apart."

"She's kinda weird."

Ava sat by herself at the end of the lunch table; her tray was barely touched.

Zayla heard the whispers. She saw the sideways glances. But instead of joining in or pretending not to notice, she made a choice.

She picked up her lunch tray and walked across the cafeteria.

"Hey," she said with a gentle smile. "Mind if I sit with you?"

Ava looked up, startled. Then… something amazing happened.

Her face changed — like the clouds in her eyes were drifting away and the sun was finally shining through.

She nodded. "Okay."

They didn't talk much at first. Just a few bites of lunch and a smile or two. But it was enough.

The next day, Zayla sat with her again. This time, she brought a joke she'd heard in class. Ava laughed — really laughed.

By the end of the week, other kids had started joining their table. Ava talked more. She walked through the hallways with her head a little higher. She raised her hand in class. She started to believe she belonged.

All because of one small, brave act.

Zayla didn't lift a car. She didn't shoot lasers from her eyes. She didn't fly.

She just saw someone who needed kindness and gave it.

And that, she realized, was the kind of superpower the world needs most.

CHAPTER 23

When They Go Low You Go

High

Bullies don't always need a reason.

Sometimes, they just want power.

And the easiest way to feel powerful is by making someone else feel small.

Zayla had seen it happen before — to other kids, to her friends, even to herself.

She knew the pattern:

They poke.

They prod.

They wait for a reaction.

Anger. Tears. Fear.

That's their win.

But one sunny afternoon in class, Zayla discovered something powerful:

You don't have to give them what they want.

It happened during quiet reading time.

Zayla had just set her books neatly on her desk, her favorite graphic novel and a poetry journal, when a boy from the next row walked by.

Without a word, he shoved the pile off her desk.

They hit the floor with a loud thud, pages flipping open like startled birds.

The room fell quiet. A few kids looked over. Waiting.

Zayla felt the heat rise in her cheeks. She wanted to yell. Her heart pounded.

She could have shouted. She could have told the teacher.

But instead… she took a deep breath.

She knelt down, picked up her books slowly, and gently dusted them off.

Then she looked up at the boy and smiled.

"Wow," she said, cheerful but calm. "You must really like my books to want them on your desk, too."

He blinked.

That was not the reaction he expected. No anger. No tears. Just… confidence.

He didn't know what to say. He shrugged and wandered off, looking a little confused.

The kids who had been watching? They were impressed. Not because Zayla yelled. But because she didn't.

After class, a girl leaned over and whispered, "That was actually kind of cool."

Zayla smiled again, this time for real.

It wasn't easy staying calm. But it made her feel strong in a way that shouting never had.

That day, Zayla learned something she'd never forget:

When someone tries to bring you down, you don't have to go with them.

When they go low, you can go high.

And when you do, everyone watching learns what real strength looks like.

Reflection:

What does Zayla's response to the bully teach us about true strength and self-control, and how can staying calm in tough moments shift the power away from those trying to hurt us?"

CHAPTER 24

You're Not Alone

Sometimes, when you're being picked on, it feels like the world gets smaller.

Like the noise around you fades, and all you can hear are the mean words.

It feels like you're standing alone on an island and no one else sees it.

But guess what?

You're not alone. Not even close.

Zayla knew what that kind of loneliness felt like. She'd been there before — when kids made fun of her for asking too many questions, or for the way she decorated her notebooks with stars and poetry.

So, when she saw a younger student being picked on one chilly morning outside the school doors, something inside her stopped.

The boy stood near the bike rack, clutching his backpack tightly. A few older kids were circling him, pointing at the patches on his coat and laughing.

"Hey, did you make that thing yourself?"

"Nice backpack, what is it, from the dinosaur age?"

The boy looked down. His face was red. He didn't say a word.

Zayla could've kept walking. A lot of people did.

But instead, she took a deep breath and walked toward him.

She didn't yell. She didn't try to fight.

She just stood beside him, tall, calm, and kind.

"Hey," she said gently, smiling at him. "You want to come hang out with us?"

The boy blinked. "Me?"

"Yeah. We're heading over to the library table before class. You can sit with us."

He hesitated… and then nodded.

The bullies, caught off guard, mumbled something and backed off. The crowd that had gathered slowly lost interest and drifted away.

Zayla led the boy over to where a few other kids were sitting, kids she knew would be kind.

"Everyone, this is Jordan," she said. "He's joining us today."

Someone slid over to make room. Another offered part of their muffin.

Jordan smiled for the first time that morning.

The next day, he came back. And the day after that.

Soon, others started joining them, too: kids who were quiet, kids who felt different, kids who had also stood alone at some point. Together, they built something strong: a group that made room for everyone.

They didn't need matching outfits or a club name.

They just had each other.

And when someone has even one person standing beside them, the island doesn't feel so lonely anymore.

Zayla realized something important:

Sometimes, it only takes one brave person to reach out…

to remind someone else they're not standing alone.

CHAPTER 25

Stronger Than You Think

The sun was warm on Zayla's shoulders as she sat outside at lunch, her tray balanced on her knees and a gentle breeze brushing her hair from her face.

She looked around, not nervously, not shyly. Just calmly.

A few kids were playing four squares. Others were laughing near the jungle gym. At a nearby table, her friends were saving her a seat. One of them waved.

Zayla waved back, but she didn't rush. She wanted to sit in this moment for a bit longer, because something had changed; she had changed.

She wasn't the same girl who once sat quietly at the edge of the playground, pretending not to hear the whispers.

She wasn't the girl who used to shrink into herself when someone gave her a mean look or called her names.

She had faced bullying, the loud kind, the sneaky kind, and even the kind that hides behind jokes.

And each time, she made a choice.

She chose to speak up.

She chose to walk away.

Stick and Stones

She chose kindness when others didn't.

She chose herself.

Every time someone tried to push her down, she used the strength inside her to rise a little taller, a little braver, a little more her. And now?

Now she wasn't just surviving school days. She was thriving.

She had friends who saw her for who she truly was: kind, creative, funny, and strong.

She had learned how to build a shield not out of silence or anger, but out of truth, boundaries, and belief in herself.

She smiled wider, heart full.

Because bullies? They might say mean things. They might try to make people feel small. But they could never touch what mattered most:

Zayla's voice.

Zayla's heart.

Zayla's worth.

And now, she knew that strength didn't come from yelling the loudest or pushing back the hardest.

It came from knowing who you are and refusing to shrink just to make someone else comfortable.

As she stood to join her friends, she took one last breath of the spring air.

This was the kind of life she had built, piece by piece, day by day, a life where she didn't need to hide.

She was stronger than she ever thought she could be.

And she was just getting started.

CHAPTER 26

Lifting Others

Zayla had come a long way.

But she wasn't the only one who needed strength.

And now… she noticed things she used to miss.

At lunch, she saw a kid sitting alone with earbuds in, staring down at their tray.

In the hallway, she spotted someone stuffing a mean note into another student's locker.

She heard quiet jokes disguised as "just teasing."

Before, she might have walked past.

Now? She paused.

Because she understood something most people didn't:

Sometimes, the smallest moments carry the biggest weight.

One morning, Zayla saw a girl in the library looking lost — not lost like she didn't know where to go, but lost in the way her shoulders slumped and her eyes flicked quickly around the room, hoping not to be noticed.

Zayla remembered that feeling.

So, she walked over and said, "Hi, I'm Zayla. Want to sit with us?"

The girl looked surprised. "You don't even know me."

Zayla smiled. "I don't have to. I just thought… maybe you didn't want to sit alone today."

They sat together. They didn't talk much, and that was okay.

Sometimes, kindness didn't need a big speech.

Sometimes, it just needed a seat.

Zayla didn't think of herself as a leader.

But others started to notice the way she acted.

The way she stood up without making a scene.

The way she helped people feel seen, really seen.

One afternoon, her teacher pulled her aside after class.

"Zayla," she said softly, "you've become someone people feel safe around. That's a kind of leadership, too."

Zayla blinked. "Me? I'm just… being nice."

The teacher smiled. "Exactly."

Zayla walked home that day thinking about those words.

She didn't have a crown. She didn't lead a club.

But she did have a voice and a story and the courage to help others feel strong, too.

And maybe, just maybe…

That was how change started.

Not with a big speech.

But with one brave, quiet person who said,

"You can sit with me."

Reflection

"How can small acts of kindness, like Zayla's, create a ripple effect in a community, and have you ever experienced or witnessed a moment like that?"

CHAPTER 27

The Pause of Pause

Some days, things just build up.

That's how it was for Zayla on Tuesday.

First, she forgot her math homework.

Then she spilled juice on her shirt at snack time.

By the time group project time rolled around, she was already frustrated and tired.

She was working with three classmates to build a poster for science. Everyone had a job… except one boy, Marcus, who just kept talking over people and drawing random things all over the poster.

"Marcus, can you please just let us focus?" Zayla asked.

He rolled his eyes. "Maybe if your idea wasn't so boring, I'd care."

Zayla's face got hot.

The old version of her — the one who used to react fast and loud — wanted to snap. Her fists clenched. Her heartbeat is faster.

But something inside her whispered:

Pause.

So, she did.

"I need a minute," Zayla said, standing up.

She walked out into the hallway and sat on the bench by the water fountain. She didn't cry. She didn't yell. She just breathed.

In through her nose.

Out through her mouth.

She counted to ten.

And then, something amazing happened: the heat in her face cooled. The pressure in her chest eased. The storm inside her started to pass.

When she walked back into the classroom, she felt lighter.

She calmly told the teacher, "Can we try switching roles in our group? I think that would help."

And it did.

Marcus, caught off guard by how calm Zayla stayed, actually listened. The group got back on track. The poster turned out great.

Later, one of her groupmates whispered, "I would've totally lost it. You handled that like a pro."

Zayla smiled. Not because everything had been perfect — but because she had been in control of herself.

That day, Zayla learned something new about strength.

It's not just about standing up for others.

Sometimes, it's about standing still and knowing when to pause before you say something you can't take back.

Reflection:

"What does Zayla's experience teach us about emotional strength and the importance of pausing before reacting, and how can taking a moment to breathe help us respond more calmly in tough situations?"

CHAPTER 28

One Compliment Can Change

Everything

Zayla knew what it felt like to be overlooked.

That's why she noticed the quiet kid in art class, the one who always sat in the back, sleeves pulled over their hands, head low, sketching silently.

Their name was Riley.

They didn't talk much. They never raised their hand. But every day, they filled their notebook with incredible drawings of dragons, forests, space worlds, and characters that looked like they belonged in movies.

No one ever really looked.

No one ever really asked.

Until one day, Zayla happened to walk by their desk as Riley flipped the page.

Zayla stopped. "Whoa. Did you draw that?"

Riley froze. "Um… yeah."

Zayla smiled widely. "That's amazing. Seriously. The shadows, the way it looks like it's moving, you're really good."

Riley blinked. "Thanks," they mumbled, a bit shocked. "I don't really show people."

"Well, you should," Zayla said. "This could go in, like, an art show."

She meant it.

Riley didn't say much more, but Zayla noticed a difference the next day. Riley sat a little straighter. Their sketchbook was out on the desk, open. And at the end of the week, when the teacher announced the school was having an art contest, Riley signed up.

Zayla saw their name on the list.

Weeks later, Riley's drawing of a glowing dragon curled around a planet hung in the hallway for everyone to see. People stopped. People stared. People noticed.

Zayla didn't brag about being the first one to compliment them. She didn't need to.

Because she had learned something important:

Kind words don't just make someone's day. Sometimes, they change someone's story.

It didn't take a crowd.

It didn't take a speech.

Just a moment, one real compliment, spoken with heart.

Zayla knew now that kindness wasn't always about big, brave actions.

Sometimes, it was as simple as saying:

"I see you. And you're amazing."

CHAPTER 29

The Day Zayla Messed Up

Zayla had learned a lot about kindness, courage, and standing up for others.

But one day, she learned something just as important:

Even she could mess up.

It started in the cafeteria.

Zayla was sitting with her usual group, joking, laughing, tossing bits of granola bar across the table like mini rockets.

That's when she saw someone walk by wearing bright purple shoes.

Not just a bright glow in the dark purple.

Without even thinking, Zayla blurted out, "Whoa! Those shoes are attacking my eyeballs!"

The kids at her table burst out laughing.

Zayla smiled — until she saw the face of the girl wearing the shoes.

Stick and Stones

Her name was Nia. She stopped mid-step, looking down at her feet.

She didn't say a word. She just hurried past, head down, tray clutched tightly in her hands.

Zayla felt a twist in her stomach.

She hadn't meant to be mean. It was just a joke, right?

But something about Nia's face stuck with her the rest of the day.

After school, Zayla sat on her bed and replayed it over and over. The joke. The laughter. The way Nia looked so small in that moment.

Zayla realized something hard:

Even if she hadn't meant to be unkind, she had been.

So, the next morning, she did something brave.

She found Nia before homeroom and gently tapped her on the shoulder.

"Hey… um, about yesterday," Zayla said. "I said something about your shoes, and I thought I was being funny, but I think I hurt your feelings. I'm sorry."

Nia blinked. "Oh."

Zayla nodded. "Your shoes are actually super cool. I wish I could pull off purple like that."

Nia gave a small smile. "They're my favorite color. My grandma got them for me."

Zayla smiled back. "She's got great taste."

They didn't become instant best friends. But something shifted in both of them.

And Zayla walked away feeling lighter.

Because now she knew:

Being kind doesn't mean being perfect.

It means listening when your heart says, "That wasn't okay."

It means fixing what you can. And meaning it.

That day, Zayla learned that real strength doesn't come from never messing up.

It comes from owning your mistakes… and choosing to do better.

CHAPTER 30

The Big Test

It was the day of the big science presentation.

Zayla stood at the front of the classroom, her hands gripping the edges of the podium a little too tightly. Her heart was racing. Her mind kept swirling with thoughts: What if I mess up? What if they laugh at me? What if they think my project is dumb?

She glanced at her project a model volcano, carefully crafted and painted, with a paper mache base that she had worked on for weeks. It looked great. It was even designed to explode (on purpose, of course), and she was proud of it.

But today wasn't about the volcano. Today was about speaking in front of the class, which still made her nervous. Even though she had grown so much in the past few months, there were still moments when her fears tried to sneak in and take over.

"Alright, Zayla, you're up," Ms. Jensen said, smiling at her from the front of the room.

Zayla took a deep breath and walked up to the front. As she began to speak, her voice wavered a little, but she quickly regained control. She explained the science behind the volcano eruption, how it was like the real thing, and what made it "explode" safely. Her classmates were watching, and Zayla could tell they were interested, not laughing.

But then she reached the part of her presentation where she needed to trigger the eruption.

Her hands trembled as she reached for the little button hidden in the volcano's base. She took another deep breath and pressed it. The volcano rumbled and then, with a dramatic burst of red liquid, it erupted.

There was a collective gasp from the class.

It was perfect.

Zayla felt her stomach flutter with pride, but she still had to finish. As the eruption calmed down, Zayla continued speaking, wrapping up her explanation. She looked around the room, meeting the eyes of her classmates. Some were grinning, others were nodding along, clearly impressed.

When she finished, the room was quiet for a moment.

Then, the applause came.

It wasn't huge or boisterous, but it was warm. Her friends clapped loudly, and even some of the quieter kids gave her a smile of approval.

Ms. Jensen gave her a thumb-up. "That was an excellent presentation, Zayla. I'm really proud of you."

Zayla felt a warm rush inside her. She had done it. She had faced her fear of speaking in front of the class, and she had done it well.

But as the class continued, Zayla realized something important:

The applause didn't feel as big as the victory inside her.

Because it wasn't the eruption that mattered most, it was the fact that she had stood there, nervous, yes, but confident enough to keep going. She hadn't let fear stop her from sharing something she loved, something she'd worked hard on. And that made her stronger than any applause.

Later, when the class was over, Zayla walked out into the hallway, her heart still a little fluttery. Her friends surrounded her, congratulating her on the presentation. But it wasn't just the volcano or the science she was proud of.

It was the way she'd faced something that scared her and turned it into a moment of growth. The way she didn't shrink back, even when the nerves almost got the best of her.

And the best part?

She knew this wasn't the last time she would face something scary and succeed.

Because Zayla had learned something important:

Strength wasn't just about being fearless. It was about having the courage to take action even when fear was still there.

She didn't need to wait for the fear to go away. She had already proven to herself that she was stronger than it.

And with that, she smiled to herself, feeling ready for whatever came next.

CHAPTER 31

Not for Sale

Zayla had always loved her style: colorful headbands, mismatched socks, and her favorite oversized hoodie that said "Kindness is Cool."

It wasn't trendy. It wasn't what the "popular" girls wore.

But it was her.

So, when a new trend swept through school, short skirts, expensive sneakers, and designer backpacks, Zayla didn't rush to join in. She liked what she liked. That used to make her nervous… but not anymore.

Until one day, during gym, two girls from the "cool" group sat on the bench near her and whispered just loud enough for her to hear.

"I mean, she could be pretty if she tried."

"Yeah. That sweatshirt again? It's, like, every day."

Zayla heard every word.

Old Zayla might've looked down at her shoes. She might've gone home and begged her mom to buy the expensive stuff, just so she'd fit in.

But not this Zayla.

This Zayla turned to them, calm and steady, and said:

"I dress for me, not for you. But thanks for your opinion."

Then she walked away and finished her stretches.

The girls looked stunned, not because she had been rude, but because she hadn't been shaken. Zayla didn't yell. She didn't explain. She didn't need to.

She knew who she was.

And that, she realized, was something no one could sell in a store or measure with labels.

Stick and Stones

At lunch that day, one of the quietest girls in class walked up to her and whispered, "I love your hoodie. I have one kinda like it at home, but I was scared to wear it."

Zayla grinned. "Wear it. You'll look awesome."

And that's when she knew:

Being yourself might not always get you approval from everyone — but it will attract the right kind of people.

People who like you for you.

That kind of confidence?

It wasn't loud.

It didn't brag.

But it was powerful.

Because Zayla wasn't just wearing confidence.

She was living it.

Reflection:

"What does Zayla's story teach us about confidence and staying true to yourself, especially when others try to make you feel like you need to change to fit in?"

CHAPTER 32

The Ripple Effect

The day started like any other until Zayla noticed something strange.

As she walked into school, someone smiled and said, "Nice backpack!"

It wasn't someone she usually talked to. But it made her smile.

So, during homeroom, she leaned over to a classmate and whispered, "You're really good at drawing."

At recess, that same classmate told another kid, "Cool shoes."

And it kept going.

By lunch, the school felt... lighter. Warmer. Like the walls had taken a deep breath.

No one had planned it. No one had posted about it. But something had started.

A ripple made of kindness.

Zayla watched it travel from one kid to the next. And she realized something important:

Kindness doesn't need a stage.

It doesn't need to shout.

It just needs to start.

And once it does?

There's no telling how far it can go.

Reflection

How does this chapter show that even small, simple acts of kindness can create big change, and what's one way you can start your own ripple of kindness in your school or community?"

CHAPTER 33

Locker Notes and Lemonade

It started as a joke. Zayla and her best friend decided to leave a sticky note inside an empty locker with a doodle that said, "You've got this!"

They laughed, wondering who might find it.

The next day, someone else left a note in a different locker:

"Don't let today mess with your sparkle."

By Friday, half the hallway was dotted with sticky notes.

Some had jokes.

Some had drawings.

Some just said, "Hi."

Nobody knew exactly who was leaving them anymore. And that was the best part.

It wasn't about being noticed.

It was about noticing others.

On Monday, the school counselor announced a "Kindness Wall" where kids could post positive messages.

And guess who helped decorate it?

Zayla. With a cup of lemonade, glitter pens, and a smile that said,

"We made this happen."

Sometimes, change doesn't start with a speech or a protest.

Sometimes, it starts with a sticky note… and a little heart.

"It wasn't about being noticed. It was about noticing others." What does this quote mean to you?

(How can we apply that mindset in our daily lives?)

Why do you think the Kindness Wall became popular at school? What does this say about what people might be needing more of?

How does this chapter challenge the idea that only big acts or loud voices can make change?

CHAPTER 34

The Apology Circle

It was a normal Thursday — until the class had a substitute teacher and someone decided it was "prank day."

Paper airplanes.

Fake fart noises.

A desk tipped over.

The class thought it was hilarious… until the substitute looked like she was about to cry.

Zayla felt something twist in her chest. This wasn't funny anymore.

The next day, their regular teacher was back — and she was not smiling.

She asked everyone to sit in a circle.

No pointing fingers. No punishments.

Just one rule:

"If you were part of the prank, even just laughing — own it. And then tell us what you'll do differently next time."

Zayla went first.

She hadn't thrown anything. But she had laughed.

"I think I hurt someone's feelings without meaning to," she said. "Next time, I'll speak up."

A few other kids followed. Some apologized. Some stayed quiet.

But by the end, something amazing happened:

The substitute teacher came back the next week.

She smiled.

She thanked the class.

And Zayla realized:

Owning your mistakes doesn't make you weak.

It makes you brave.

Reflection Questions

1. What did Zayla do during the prank?
2. Was it kind or unkind?
3. Why do you think Zayla chose to speak up, even though she didn't throw anything?
4. Have you ever laughed at something that might have hurt someone else's feelings?
5. How did it make you feel afterward?
6. What would you do if you saw a classmate being pranked or teased?
7. Why do you think it's brave to say "I'm sorry" or admit a mistake?
8. What are some kind things you can do to help someone feel better after a mistake has been made?

CHAPTER 35
Change Starts Quietly

It started with a note.

Folded neatly, slid into Zayla's locker between classes.

She opened it carefully and read:

"Thanks for speaking up in the circle. I was scared to say anything, but you made it feel safe."

There was no name. Just a doodle of a sun in the corner.

Zayla stared at it for a long time.

Someone had been watching. Listening.

And maybe, quietly, they were growing too.

From that day on, things felt… different.

In small ways.

Like when Jamal, the class clown, offered to help clean up after art.

Or when Ava, who used to sit alone, invited someone to join her for lunch.

Or when Sasha, the same girl who used to whisper and gossip, asked Zayla, "How are you, really?"

It wasn't perfect.

There were still off days.

Still eye rolls. Still moments when kindness didn't come easy.

But the difference?

Now, kindness had momentum.

One afternoon, Ms. Reyes pulled Zayla aside after class.

"I've noticed something," she said. "This classroom feels... different. Warmer. Quieter. Safer. You've been a big part of that."

Zayla blinked. "Me?"

"Yes, you," Ms. Reyes smiled. "You lead by example. You've created space for others to be better not by being perfect, but by being real."

Zayla didn't know what to say.

So, she just smiled.

Later that day, she watched Leo help someone pick up their spilled backpack.

She saw Ben offering to share his ruler.

She saw Nia, yes, Nia, gently telling a classmate, "Hey, don't say that. It's not kind."

These weren't huge moments.

But they were real.

They were ripples spreading out from small choices, reaching farther than anyone could see.

Zayla walked home with her hoodie sleeves pushed up, the breeze on her arms, and her heart full.

The note still sat tucked into her backpack.

It reminded her that sometimes, the loudest change starts with the quietest courage.

And Zayla knew:

She wasn't just surviving middle school.

She was helping reshape it.

💥 Reflection Questions

"This chapter shows how small acts of courage and kindness can create a ripple effect. What does Zayla's experience teach us about the quiet ways we can influence others, and how can you be someone who helps create a safer, kinder space even when no one is watching?"

CHAPTER 36

The New Kid Rule

The moment the new kid walked into the classroom, the energy shifted.

He had on a jacket two sizes too big, his hair stuck up in the back like he'd rushed to get ready, and he didn't say a word when Ms. Reyes introduced him.

Stick and Stones

"Class, this is Mateo. He's just moved here. Let's make him feel welcome."

There were a few polite nods, a few mumbled "hey," and one quiet giggle from the corner.

Zayla didn't say anything at first. She just watched.

Mateo kept his eyes down all morning.

He sat alone at lunch.

When someone bumped into him on purpose in the hallway, he didn't even react. He just kept walking.

Zayla felt something stir in her chest, something familiar.

That used to be her.

That was her, not long ago.

After lunch, she caught up with Mateo near the lockers. He looked surprised when she smiled at him.

"Hey," she said. "I'm Zayla. Wanna walk with me to class?"

Mateo nodded, but he didn't say anything.

That was okay.

She didn't need him to talk.

She just needed him to know he wasn't invisible.

The next day, she saved him a seat during group work.

The day after that, she invited him to help paint the Kindness Wall for Peer Leaders.

By Friday, Mateo said his first full sentence to her:

"I like your hoodie."

Zayla grinned. "Thanks. It's my favorite."

That afternoon, she walked into Ms. Reyes' room after school with an idea written on a notecard:

"The New Kid Rule: No one eats alone. No one gets left out. Ever."

Ms. Reyes read it, then looked at Zayla.

"You want to make this a real rule?"

"A real tradition," Zayla said. "Something we do, not just say."

And that's exactly what happened.

They made posters. They made buddy passes. They even started a student lunch squad, kids who would sit with anyone, any time, just to make sure no one felt forgotten.

By next week, Mateo wasn't the "new kid" anymore.

He was just Mateo.

And Zayla?

She realized something powerful:

Belonging doesn't happen by accident.

Sometimes, someone has to build it.

And now, she knew how.

✵ Reflection Questions

1. Why do you think Zayla noticed Mateo when others didn't? What does that say about her character?
2. Have you ever been the "new kid" or seen someone else in that position? How did it feel, and how did others respond?
3. What does the story teach us about how small actions like walking with someone or saving them a seat can make a big difference?
4. Zayla turned her idea into a tradition. Why do you think traditions like "The New Kid Rule" are important in a school or community?

5. What's the difference between being friendly and making sure someone truly belongs? Can you think of examples from your own life?

CHAPTER 37

Even Heroes Need Help

Zayla was tired.

Not the kind of tired a nap could fix.

The kind of tired that builds up slowly after too many late nights, too many responsibilities, and trying a little too hard to be "the strong one" all the time.

She was helping with Peer Leaders.

She was checking in on friends.

She was keeping up with homework and group projects, and her little brother's birthday was coming up this weekend.

And now, she had a science test she hadn't studied for.

That morning, as she stared at her messy binder and the blank study guide in her lap, her eyes stung.

She hadn't cried in a long time.

But this wasn't a loud kind of sadness. It was the quiet kind, the kind that sat in her chest like a heavy backpack no one else could see.

That's when Ms. Reyes walked by and noticed her sitting quietly before class.

"Hey," she said gently. "You, okay?"

Zayla opened her mouth to say, I'm fine.

But the words didn't come.

Instead, she looked down and whispered, "I think I'm overwhelmed."

Ms. Reyes nodded. "You've been carrying a lot lately. Want to talk?"

Zayla nodded.

They sat in the back of the classroom for five minutes before the bell. Zayla didn't say everything. But she said enough.

"I love helping," she admitted. "But I feel like if I stop for even a second, everything might fall apart."

Ms. Reyes smiled softly. "Here's the thing no one tells you: strong people still need breaks. And brave people? They ask for help."

Zayla let the words sink in.

That day, she asked her science teacher for an extra day to finish her study guide. He said yes.

She told her Peer Leaders team she needed to step back from decorating for the next event. They handled it.

She even let her mom know she was feeling stretched thin.

And something amazing happened:

The world didn't fall apart.

It kept spinning.

People understood.

People helped.

That night, Zayla wrote in her journal:

"Strength doesn't mean doing everything.

It means knowing when you can't and saying so."

She curled up under her blanket, feeling lighter.

Because sometimes the bravest thing you can say is just two small words:

"I need."

✻ Reflection Questions

1. Why is it sometimes hard to ask for help, even when we really need it?
2. What did Zayla learn about strength and bravery, and how did it change the way she handled her responsibilities?
3. Can you think of a time when you felt overwhelmed? What helped you feel supported, and what could you do differently next time?

CHAPTER 38

Different, Not Less

Zayla had seen Jordan around before.

He was quiet. He didn't always follow directions the same way everyone else did. Sometimes he covered his ears during loud assemblies or paced during group work.

Some kids called him "weird." Others just ignored him.

But Zayla noticed something different.

Jordan was brilliant with numbers. He could solve a math puzzle in seconds. He made tiny origami animals during free time, folding with lightning speed and focus. He smiled widely when someone talked to him like a friend, not like a project.

One day during gym, the class was told to form teams for relay races.

Jordan ended up last. Again.

"Do we have to have him on our team?" one kid whispered, not quietly enough.

Zayla felt that now-familiar twist in her chest.

"No," she said, stepping forward. "You get to have him. Jordan's fast. Watch."

The teacher started the stopwatch, and Jordan, who usually didn't talk much, darted across the court, beating the record by a full second.

Everyone blinked.

Zayla smiled at him. "Told you."

That afternoon, she asked Ms. Reyes about him. "Does he have autism?" she asked gently.

Ms. Reyes nodded. "He does. He processes things differently, not better or worse. Just... differently."

Zayla thought about that. Then she asked something she'd never asked before:

"What can we do better?"

Ms. Reyes beamed. "That question? That's where real inclusion begins."

The next day, Zayla brought it up during the Peer Leaders meeting.

"I think we talk about kindness a lot," she said. "But what about understanding? What about kids who feel left out even when no one's being 'mean'?"

They all sat a little straighter.

And from that conversation, something new began — posters about neurodiversity, classroom tips for inclusive group work, even a "quiet corner" in the classroom for students who needed breaks without feeling weird.

Later that week, Jordan handed Zayla a tiny paper crane.

She smiled and held it gently. "Thanks."

He didn't say anything. He didn't have to.

Because Zayla had learned something that day:

Kindness is doing the right thing.

Inclusion is making sure everyone belongs.

And just because someone's voice isn't loud…

Doesn't mean it isn't worth hearing.

💥 Reflection Questions

What does Zayla's story teach us about the difference between being kind and being inclusive, and how can we make sure everyone in our own communities feels like they truly belong?"

CHAPTER 39

The Apology Circle

The last week of school always felt strange.

Boxes lined the classroom walls.

The whiteboard was nearly empty.

Everyone buzzed with summer plans and yearbook signings and "remember when" stories.

Zayla sat at her desk, her fingers brushing the inside cover of her notebook.

It was the same notebook she'd had at the beginning of the year, the one where she used to scribble poems in the margins, hoping no one noticed her.

The one where she once wrote:

"Maybe if I stay small, they won't see me."

Now the pages were full.

Not just with poems but with notes, ideas, plans, and reflections.

Moments that used to feel small but now felt… huge.

She thought back:

To the day she stood beside someone being teased instead of walking by.

To the time she accepted Sasha's apology, even if things never went back to perfect.

To the kindness wall. The apology circle. The moment she realized that even she needed help sometimes.

Zayla had been the quiet kid.

Then the kind kid.

Then the brave kid.

Now?

She was still all those things and more.

She'd learned that strength wasn't about being the loudest.

It was about knowing what mattered and standing by it.

She'd learned that kindness wasn't just lovely, it was powerful.

That walking away from drama was sometimes the boldest move of all.

And she'd learned that even the smallest voice can change a room, a class, maybe even a whole school if it speaks with truth.

Zayla looked up at her friends across the room. Some were waving goodbye. Others were laughing. One of them caught her eye and smiled.

She smiled back.

Not nervously. Not shyly. Just… calmly.

Because Zayla knew now:

She wasn't "becoming" someone.

She already was someone.

And she was ready for whatever came next.

❋ Reflection Questions

1. At the beginning of the year, Zayla wanted to "stay small." What do you think that means? Have you ever felt that way?
2. How did Zayla's notebook help show how much she had changed by the end of the year?
3. What were some of the brave things Zayla did this year? Which one inspired you the most? Why?
4. Zayla learned that even the smallest voice can change a room.
5. What's something you could speak up about if it really mattered to you?

6. What does it mean to be a "people leader" like Zayla? Can you think of a time when you helped someone feel seen or supported?
7. What is one thing you've learned or one way you've grown this school year that makes you proud?

CHAPTER 40

This Is Just the Beginning

The gym was buzzing with excitement.

Folding chairs lined the floor, kids fanned themselves with program sheets, and the school band played a slightly off-key version of "Don't Stop Believing."

It was the last assembly of the year, and no one expected what came next.

Ms. Reyes stepped onto the stage and tapped the mic.

"Before we go," she said, "we want to recognize someone who has quietly, consistently made this school better not with big speeches or popularity, but with courage, empathy, and real leadership."

Zayla blinked.

Wait… what?

"We call her a Peer Leader," Ms. Reyes continued. "But really, she's been a people leader. Someone who helped others stand tall just by standing beside them."

"Zayla Carter, would you join me on stage?"

Stick and Stones

Everything went quiet for half a second.

Then applause.

Then cheering.

Zayla's heart pounded as she stood. Her hands were shaking, but her feet were steady.

As she walked up to the stage, she passed classmates who used to whisper about her. Tease her. Ignore her.

Now?

They were clapping.

She turned to face the crowd, lights hot on her skin, the mic in front of her.

She didn't have a speech. But she didn't need one.

She took a breath and said:

"I used to think being strong meant staying silent. Or staying small. But now I know… strength is using your voice not to shout, but to speak up when it matters. And kindness? It's not a weakness. It's how things change."

There was a pause.

Then a standing ovation.

Zayla stepped down, cheeks warm, but heart glowing.

That afternoon, as she packed up the last of her locker, the doodles, the crumpled poems, the old name tags from Peer Leaders, she smiled to herself.

She had made mistakes. She had been afraid.

But she had grown.

Not into someone else but into herself.

And the best part?

This wasn't the end.

It was only the beginning of everything she could be.

Because kindness is a superpower.

And Zayla Carter?

She was just getting started.

Author's Notes
By Tee Soulful, M.Ed.

As someone with a master's degree in education, I've seen firsthand how bullying leaves marks far deeper than the eye can see. It doesn't just hurt feelings; it can chip away at confidence, silence voices, and impact a child's learning, social life, and mental health for years to come.

This book was written with a mission: to give students like Zayla a voice, and to give every reader a chance to reflect, grow, and stand up, whether for themselves or for someone else. Each chapter mixes humor and heart because healing doesn't have to be heavy, and sometimes the biggest lessons come wrapped in giggles and grit.

To every student who's ever felt alone, misunderstood, or left out, I see you.

You matter. Your story matters. And you deserve a world that treats you like it.

Let's make that world together.

Tee Soulful M.Ed.